**To Mary Beth,
who replaced football as my greatest love**

—M. S.

**To Charlie Nelson,
the ultimate sports fan**

—T. R.

Henry Holt and Company, LLC, *Publishers since 1866*
115 West 18th Street, New York, New York 10011

Henry Holt is a registered trademark of Henry Holt and Company, LLC

Text copyright © 1996 by Michael Sampson
Illustrations copyright © 1996 by Ted Rand
All rights reserved.
Published in Canada by Fitzhenry & Whiteside Ltd.,
195 Allstate Parkway, Markham, Ontario L3R 4T8.

Library of Congress Cataloging-in-Publication Data
Sampson, Michael. The football that won . . . / Michael Sampson;
illustrated by Ted Rand.
1. Super Bowl (Football game)—Juvenile literature. I. Rand, Ted, ill. II. Title.
GV956.2.S8S25   1996   796.332'648—dc20   95-41257

ISBN 0-8050-6312-9 / First Owlet paperback edition—1999
First published in hardcover in 1996 by Henry Holt and Company
Printed in the United States of America on acid-free paper. ∞
10 9 8 7 6 5 4 3 2 1

The artist used carbon pencil, grease pencil, and acrylic on 100 percent
cold-pressed rag stock to create the illustrations for this book.

THE FOOTBALL THAT WON...

MICHAEL SAMPSON

ILLUSTRATED BY TED RAND

HENRY HOLT AND COMPANY • NEW YORK

This is the football
That won the Super Bowl.

This is the quarterback
That fumbled the football
That won the Super Bowl.

This is the safety
That crunched the quarterback
That fumbled the football
That won the Super Bowl.

This is the touchdown
That was scored by the safety
That crunched the quarterback
That fumbled the football
That won the Super Bowl.

These are the Cowboys
That celebrated the touchdown
That was scored by the safety
That crunched the quarterback
That fumbled the football
That won the Super Bowl.

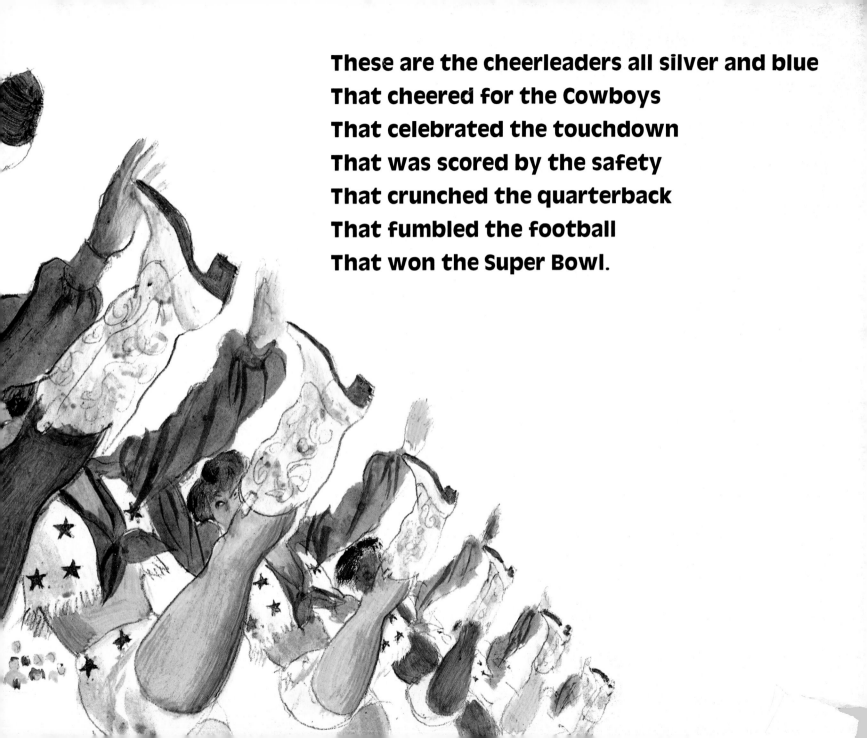

These are the cheerleaders all silver and blue
That cheered for the Cowboys
That celebrated the touchdown
That was scored by the safety
That crunched the quarterback
That fumbled the football
That won the Super Bowl.

This is the coach who shouted "Ya-hoo!"
That yelled with the cheerleaders all silver and blue
That cheered for the Cowboys
That celebrated the touchdown
That was scored by the safety
That crunched the quarterback
That fumbled the football
That won the Super Bowl.

These are the fans ninety thousand and two
That loved the coach who shouted "Ya-hoo!"
That yelled with the cheerleaders all silver and blue
That cheered for the Cowboys
That celebrated the touchdown
That was scored by the safety
That crunched the quarterback
That fumbled the football
That won the Super Bowl.

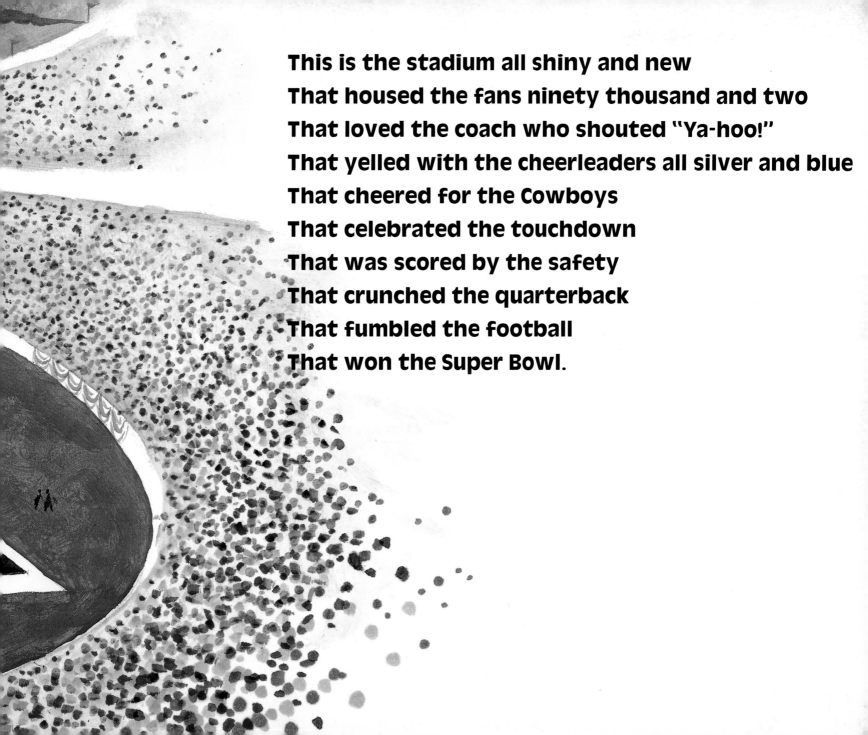

This is the stadium all shiny and new
That housed the fans ninety thousand and two
That loved the coach who shouted "Ya-hoo!"
That yelled with the cheerleaders all silver and blue
That cheered for the Cowboys
That celebrated the touchdown
That was scored by the safety
That crunched the quarterback
That fumbled the football
That won the Super Bowl.

This is the blimp that floated and flew
And circled the stadium all shiny and new
That housed the fans ninety thousand and two
That loved the coach who shouted "Ya-hoo!"
That yelled with the cheerleaders all silver and blue
That cheered for the Cowboys
That celebrated the touchdown
That was scored by the safety
That crunched the quarterback
That fumbled the football
That won the Super Bowl.

This is the Super Bowl story so true,
That was filmed by the blimp as it floated and flew
And circled the stadium all shiny and new
That housed the fans ninety thousand and two
That loved the coach who shouted "Ya-hoo!"
That yelled with the cheerleaders all silver and blue
That cheered for the Cowboys
That celebrated the touchdown
That was scored by the safety
That crunched the quarterback
That fumbled the football
That won the Super Bowl.

These are the Super Bow

amps, one and all.

And the Super Bowl trophy, crowned with the ball!